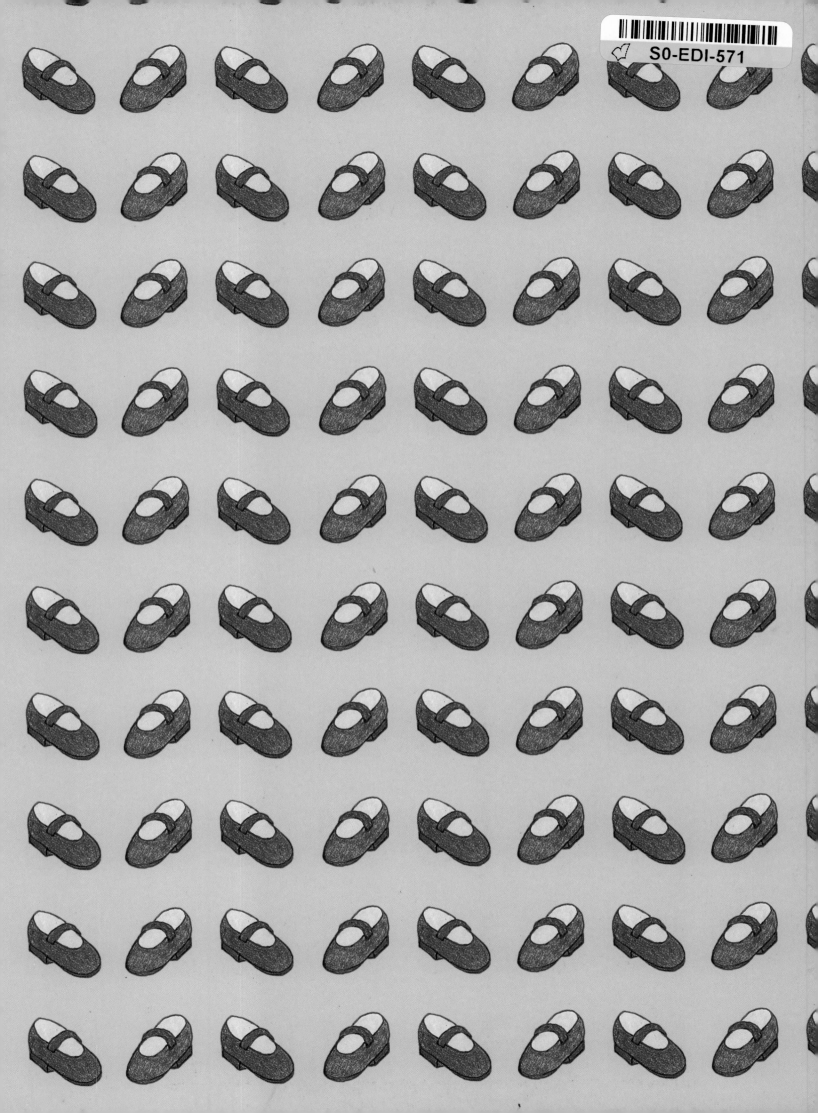

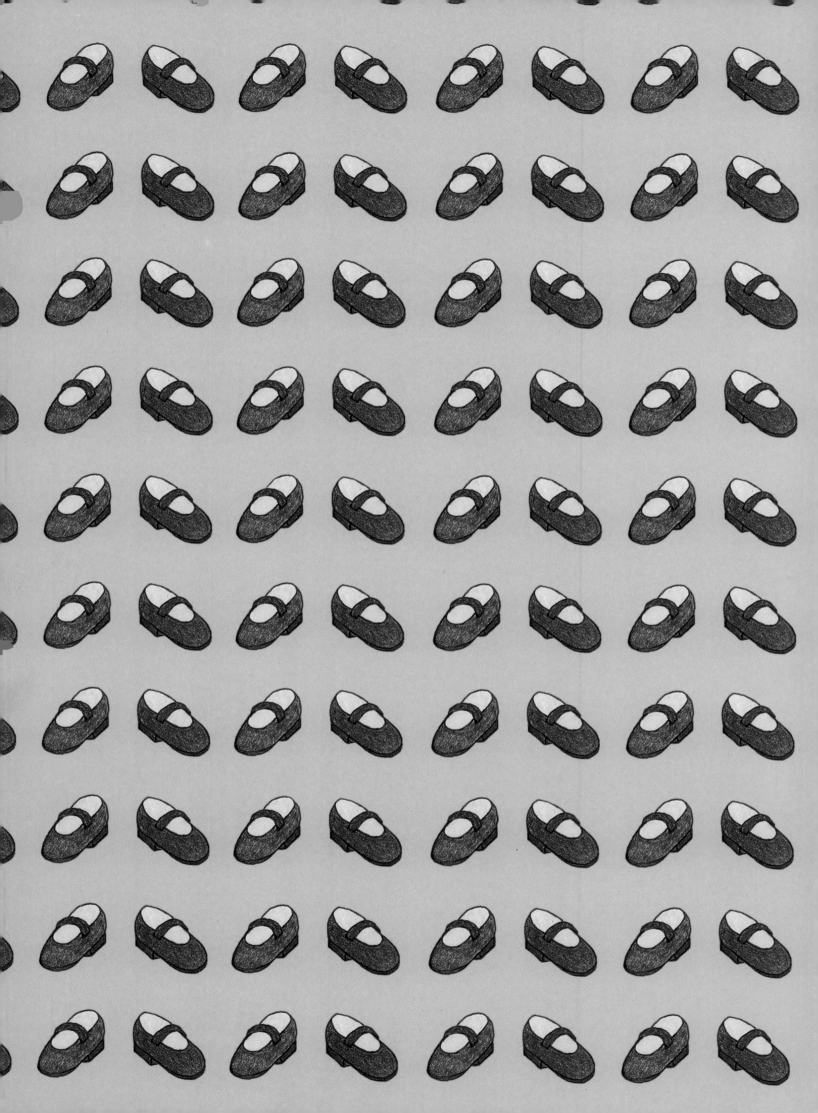

Kitty in the City

by Kinsley Foster

with illustrations by
Kari McGaren

what's inside press. ...

To my mother, for teaching me the virtues of being a lady.

Story and Illustration copyright © 1998 by Kinsley Foster

Library of Congress Catalog Card Number
98-090797

Library of Congress Cataloging-in-Publication
Data available.

Printed in Singapore

ISBN 0-9667634-0-8
10 9 8 7 6 5 4 3 2 1
First Edition

What's Inside Press
P.O. Box 16965
Beverly Hills, CA 90209

My name is Kittredge Isabella Calloway, but you may call me Kitty. I live in New York City.

This is my apartment building. I live in the very top
floor, in the penthouse.

It is very luxurious.

This is Rupert, my chauffeur. He drives me to school.

And other places too...

Tomorrow is Mother's birthday. I simply must get
her a gift. Something fabulous!

Rupert shall drive. *Merci* Rupert.

Perhaps some window shopping first.

Oooh…perfume! Mother simply adores perfume.

Ah - ah - ah…CHOO!

I am sorry Madame, but none of these tickle my fancy. Perhaps… a hat.

This one looks positively divine!

Hey! Who turned out the lights? Silly me, Mother
has plenty of hats.

Perhaps some flatware…or maybe a vase.

Woe is me. Mother simply has...everything!

But I sure could use this adorable pink dress. I *am* here to shop for mother, but I suppose it wouldn't hurt to put it on hold until tomorrow.

Maybe a light lunch will help to clear my thoughts… I would like a cucumber sandwich, *s'il vous plaît*, and a Kitty cocktail. You simply musn't be shy with the cherries. *Merci Garçon!*

19

I must say, finger sandwiches are divine… One
chicken croissant to go please. *Merci!*

Jewelry is positively my last hope! If only Mother
wore costume, it is quite affordable.

21

Thank you very much Madame, but I am afraid
none of these are quite special enough for Mother.

Fiddle dee dee Rupert. I am quite empty handed,
except for your croissant. You must be simply
famished!

Thank you Miss Kitty. And remember, the very best gifts come from the heart.

Rupert is right! I can make something for Mother.

La, la, la! Chocolate is Mother's favorite. Mine too.

Mother simply adored it!

THE END

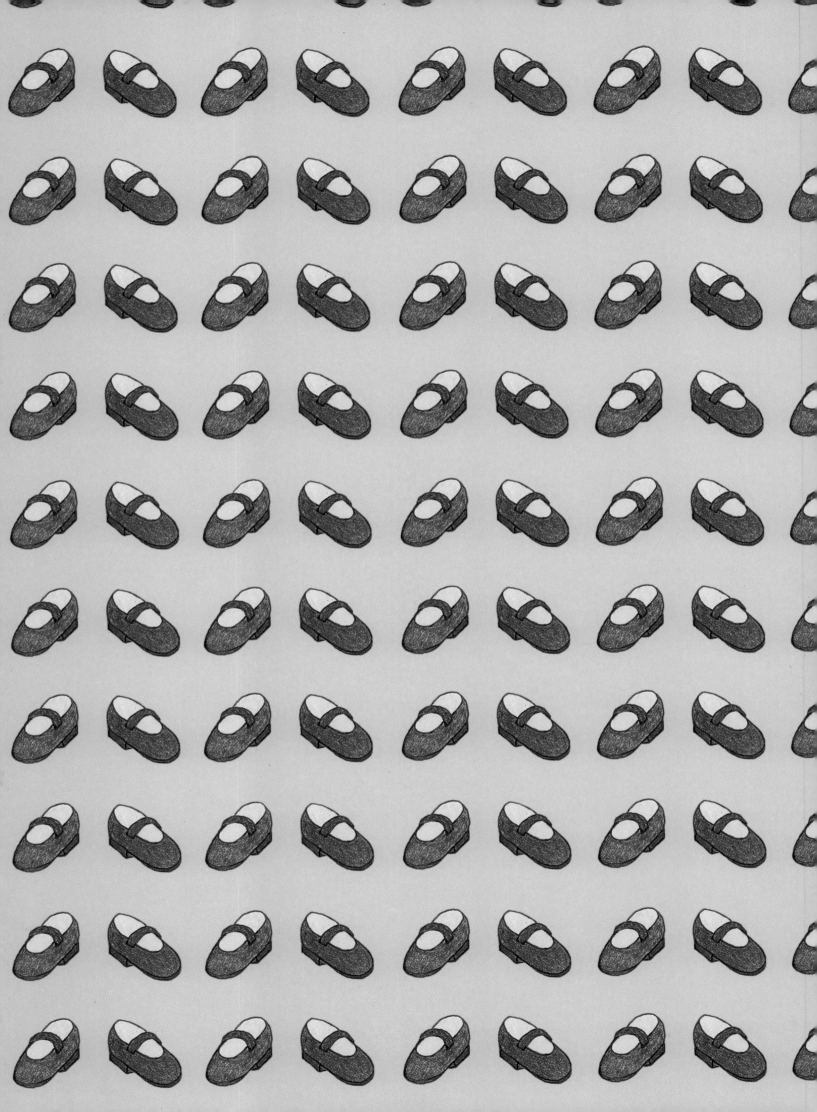

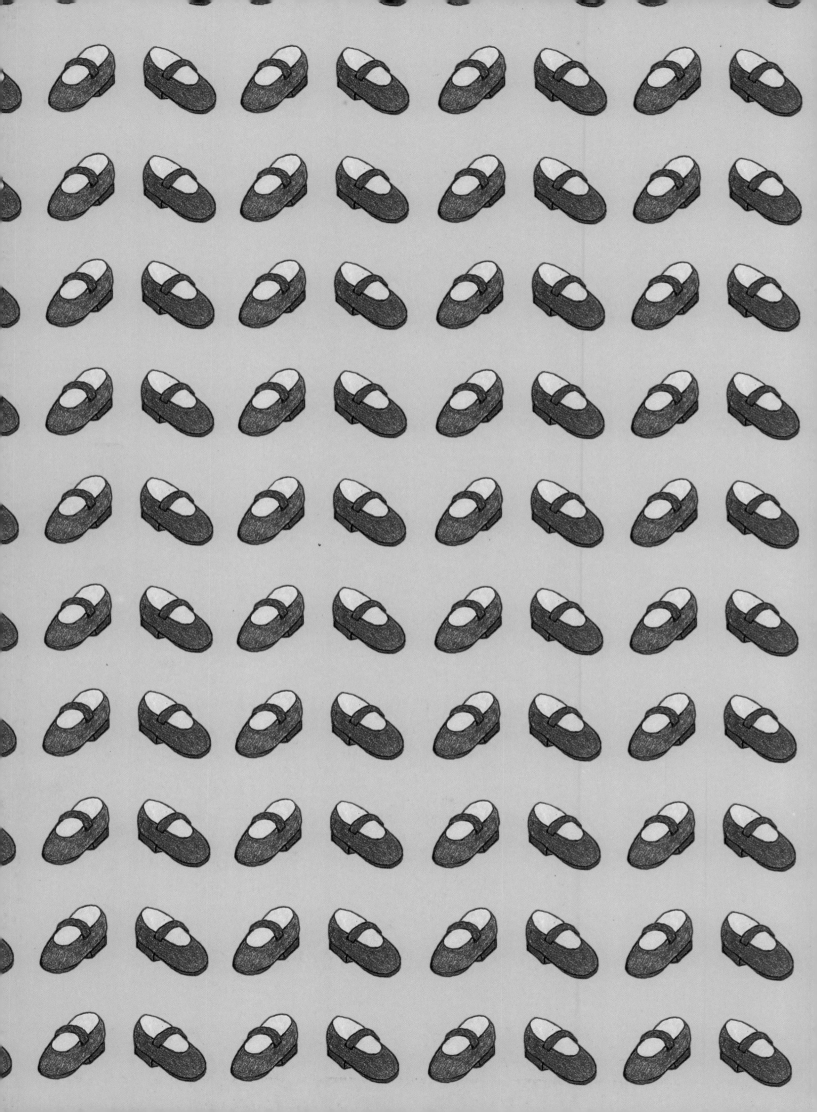